Dancing in the Rain

Written and Illustrated by Dee Smith

Copyright © 2016

Visit Deesignery.com

Others hurry inside but I hurry out.

I hurry out to join the rain.

I am dancing.

I am spinning.

I am smiling.

I am dancing in the rain.

The trees are softly swaying.

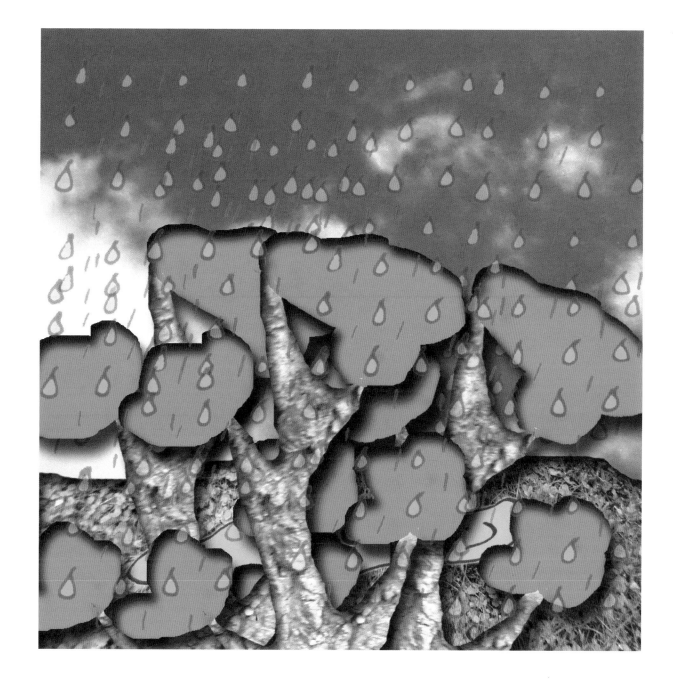

They are dancing too.

I feel the soft water splashing on my skin.

My hair hugs my face.

The sky's tears of joy slide down my hands.

They land lovingly at my feet.

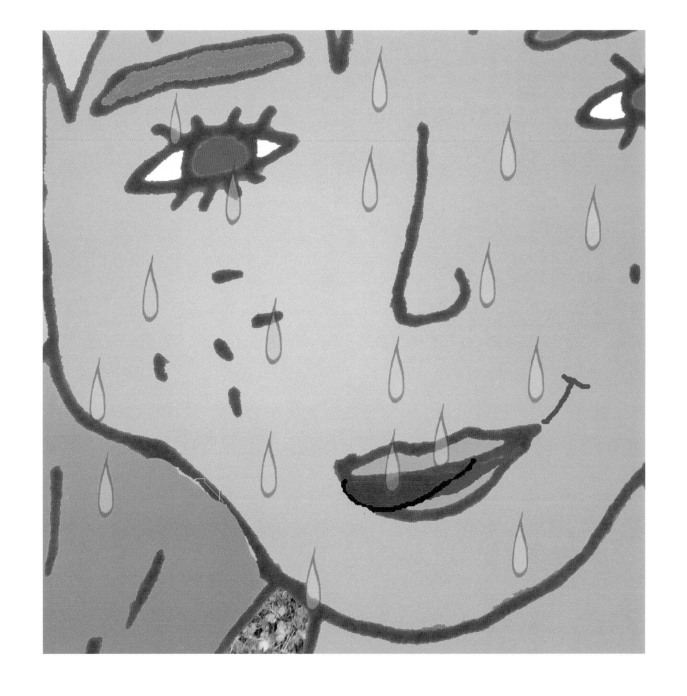

I stick my tongue out to catch a few droplets.

They taste sweet and salty.

I jump in a puddle.

The water flies towards me.

It joins me in an embrace.

I love the dance.

I love the rain.

Oh what a beautiful day!

Dedicated to all those with rainy days.

Thank You!

Thank you so much for reading this book.
It means the world to me!
If you liked the book I would much appreciate if you would write a Review on Amazon. I am so thankful for each and every person supporting my dream of being a writer for children. Because you have read this book, yes that means YOU too! Thanks Again!
Stay tuned for more titles on my website Deesignery.com

Regards,
Dee

About the Author:

My name is Dee Smith. I am an Author and Illustrator. My hobbies include graphic design, puppetry, balloon twisting, drawing and of course writing. I am dedicated to my mission of keeping children both protected and entertained in fun and innovative ways.

DEESIGNERY.COM

Made in the USA
Charleston, SC
31 March 2016